A retired Orthopaedic S   ⎯
retirement and has self-published on Amazon. His books
cover the wide range of human experiences and
emotions.

The Shard

Martin Nelson

The Shard

Vanguard Press

A CIP catalogue record for this title is
available from the British Library.

ISBN 978 1 80016 506 9

*Vanguard Press is an imprint of
Pegasus Elliot Mackenzie Publishers Ltd.*
www.pegasuspublishers.com

First Published in 2023

**Vanguard Press
Sheraton House Castle Park
Cambridge England**

Printed & Bound in Great Britain

To Diana, always in my heart

Prologue

A young girl finds a broken piece of crockery in her garden in Georgia, USA. It has a series of parallel lines incised into it, a design that can be traced back to her ancestors — enslaved Africans brought to the USA from West Africa in the 1800s. She takes it to show her mother who doesn't know how it got there.

Years later, when clearing out the family home, she comes upon it. She wants to understand how it got into the garden. In doing so she uncovers a story of greed and cruelty.

Chapter One

The Discovery of the Shard

Bikita couldn't now remember when she first found it. She had travelled home to see her mother who was recovering after a fall.

'Hi Mum,' Bikita called out as she let herself into the house.

Both she and her brother Abraham had keys, so that in the event of a problem, they could both get into the house.

'I'm upstairs,' her mother had called out. Climbing the stairs, she met Abraham at the top.

'How is she?' Bikita whispered, nodding to the bedroom.

'Not good, she's very weak. You will see for yourself. I am sorry I can't stay longer but I must get back to sort out some problems at the factory.'

They hugged.

'Thanks for staying. I'm sorry I couldn't get here sooner.'

He shrugged and was gone. Bikita pushed the bedroom door open and went in. Stale air hit her, and she immediately went to open the windows.

'No, no leave them,' her mother murmured. 'It's so cold when they're open. Come and sit down beside me.'

Bikita hadn't seen her mother for some time and was horrified by her appearance. She had shrunk and was now no bigger than a ten-year old child. The skin on her face had retracted clearly outlining the bones of her skull. Her eyes, sunken in their sockets, looked out weary and tired. Bikita reached out and held her hand. Her fingers were clammy with hardly any flesh.

'What happened, Mum?'

'It was so stupid. You know how I love the garden. Well, it was a lovely sunny day and I felt really well so I decided to clean out the greenhouse. It was in a terrible state after the winter and needed attention. I couldn't resist the challenge. I was on a ladder reaching up to cut down that dead grapevine that so annoys me when I slipped and came crashing down. I didn't feel any pain at first and thought I was fine until I tried to get up and then I realised something was wrong. My right leg was twisted beneath me. My neighbour must have heard me cry out because he came to my help very quickly. The X-rays confirmed that I had broken my hip. I had the operation the same day and came home about four days ago. Abraham has been wonderful. He came immediately and has been an angel.

'How are you feeling now?' asked Bikita.

'Not good but, Bikita, you must help me. I can't just lie here, I must get up, I have so much to do.'

Bikita thought for a moment. She phoned her office.

'Hi, its Bikita, can I speak to the boss?'

There was a pause and then a man's voice, 'Hello Bi, when are you coming back? I've got a great story for you.'

'Mmm! Hi, Boss, it's difficult. Mum is really not very well. She is very weak after the fall and her op and…'

'What are you saying?'

'I need another week.'

'Oh Hell! Okay, one week — no more. Then I want you back here, do you understand?'

'Thanks, Boss, see you in a week.'

Bikita turned to her mother. 'I can stay another week, then I must be back or I'll lose my job.'

They sat in silence, the only sound a ticking clock.

Then, 'How are you?' her mother's voice rasped, her words rattling in her throat.

'Fine, I'm fine now. The divorce was messy, so many incriminations but it's all over now.'

'What are your plans?'

'Plans? Umm, I don't know, I'm thinking of writing a book.'

'A book?'

'Yes, about the shard. Don't you remember?'

'Oh yes, the shard. You were a child at the time weren't you? Probably no more than five years' old, our first child as your brother hadn't yet been born. We had named you Bikita, a Bantu name in memory of your great, great grandparents. We were living in an old Georgian house in one of the southern states. I think it was early spring, the weather was beginning to improve so I had allowed you to play out in the garden. Do you remember, you used to love to run around it, saying that it was enormous, a whole world of your own? But years later you realised that it wasn't very large at all although still big enough for you to explore.

You had been rummaging in the back along the rear hedge when you found it. It was half sticking out of the ground and at first you said you thought that it was a stone but then you saw the faint markings. Excited, you rushed in shouting,

'Look, Mummy, look what I've found. It was in the garden at the back.'

You handed it to me. It was covered in mud.

'Bikita, it's dirty, dear,' I said, taking it from you and preparing to throw it away.

'No! It's mine, I want to keep it,' you cried, trying to tear it away from my grasp.

'Darling, it's dirty.'

Then I noticed some faint lines on it. I took it to the tap and washed away some of the soil. The markings became clearer. They looked like parallel thin lines with a regular pattern.

Finally, I recognised what it was.

'It's a shard, a piece of broken crockery.'

'Where do you think it came from?' you asked.

I took your hand. 'Darling, you are too young to understand how it got there. Why don't you keep it and one day when you're older, you can learn more about it? Put it in your box, the one in which you keep all your treasures.'

Sometime later, after her mother's death, Bikita was clearing out the house. It was full of her things, and she

13

hated throwing anything away. Most of her clothes had been packed up, ready to go to the charity shop and Bikita was beginning to sort out the furniture. Going through the drawers, she came upon the shard. She turned it over in her hands. For a moment she was confused. What was it and why had it been kept and not thrown away? She thought for a moment and then she remembered. She was once again that five-year-old holding the broken shard. She stopped and sat, fighting back her tears.

It was later when Bikita was standing in the garden looking down at the place where she had found it so many years earlier that she remembered her mother's words.

It was then that she decided to learn all she could about it. She needed to know how it had got there. She suspected it was going to be a difficult journey into her past. A journey that would take her to places she may never have heard of and to meet people who were her distant cousins in a faraway country.

Chapter Two

Shades of Brown

Bikita returned to New York — where she was working in a newspaper office, a small, local journal mainly dealing with domestic matters — and forgot about the shard. But not for long. She was preparing an article on the challenges facing families who had recently moved into the district and had arranged to visit the Douglas' family who had relocated there less than three months earlier.

Arriving at their address, Bikita saw a car in the drive and assumed that the family were at home. She walked up to the front door, knocked and waited. The door was opened by a young Afro-American woman.

'Hi, I'm Bikita Trimingham, a journalist.' And then without thinking, 'Is Mrs Douglas at home?'

'Hi, I'm her,' she replied with a smile.

Embarrassed, Bikita stuttered, 'I'm sorry I...

'It's okay, it happens all the time. People think I'm the house-help. Please come in, Bikita. My name is Lysha, how can I help you?'

'I'm writing a piece on the challenges facing Afro-American homeowners coming into the area.'

Lysha smiled.

'You have just met one. So many people assume that all people of colour are servants.'

Bikita flushed.

'I don't know what to say. I feel so ashamed, being Afro-American myself.'

'Afro-American? But you're white.'

'Yes, Lysha, you see you have the same confusion. My great, great, grandparents came from West Africa as slaves.'

'Wow, Bikita!' said Lysha — they were now on first-name terms. 'No wonder we all get confused. Perhaps one day we will all be shades of brown and no one will judge us by the colour of our skin.'

Chapter Three

The Shard

While they were talking, Bikita was glancing around the room admiring the decor.

'What a lovely room you have.'

'Thank you.'

In the corner she saw a display cabinet containing what looked like some unusual objects.

'Do you mind if I have a look?'

'No please do. My husband and I like to collect things from places we have visited.'

Bikita walked over to the cabinet and looked more closely at the many items displayed. She suddenly stopped. On the middle shelf, there was a simple, plain clay bowl. It was in its natural colour with a long crack down one side that had been skilfully repaired. What caught her attention was the decoration.

'That bowl? May I look at it?' Bikita asked.

'Yes, please do. I'll get it out.'

Lysha took a small key and opened the cabinet door. Reaching in, she took out the bowl and handed it to Bikita. She could see the surprise on Bikita's face.

'Bikita, what's got you so excited?'

A series of parallel lines had been etched into its surface. Bikita stared at them and suddenly remembered. They were the same as she had seen on her shard.

'It's the markings. See those parallel lines? They are the same as the ones on my shard.'

'Your shard?'

'I'm sorry, I didn't tell you. Let me explain.'

Over the next twenty minutes, Bikita told Lysha how she had found a shard in their garden many years before.

Finally, she asked, 'Where did you get your bowl?'

'It's my husband; he's the collector. I just like interesting things. I'll ask him when he gets home. Let me have your cell number and I will call you.'

Later that day, her phone rang.

'Hi Bikita, it's me,' Lysha said. 'I spoke to my husband. He can't recall. He says it's been in his family for as long as he can remember. He is going to make some enquiries.'

Chapter Four

Visiting West Africa

At last Bikita had managed to get some leave but she couldn't go until she had found a temporary home for Tabby, her cat. Tabby had just turned up one day and it was love at first sight. They had now been together for almost four years.

Holding Tabby in her arms, she knocked on her next-door neighbour's door and waited. She heard the sound of feet and suddenly the door was opened by Penelope, her neighbour's six-year-old daughter.

'Hi Penny, is Mummy or Daddy at home?'

'Hi Bi. No, I'm here on my own.'

'Look, I'm in a bit of a hurry. Do you think Mummy and Daddy would mind looking after Tabby for me.? I've got to go away for a few weeks.'

'Tabby? That's our Ginger you're holding.'

Once they had sorted out the confusion and agreed that they both owned the cat or perhaps neither of them did, Bikita was free to go.

Hartsfield-Jackson airport, Atlanta was Bikita's nearest airport to Kinshasa. It was a twenty-minute drive from her home through open countryside. Then as she entered the city, the traffic began to increase. Reaching the airport, she parked her car and entered the terminal. She had only been there once before so was at first confused by the signage. Looking down the list of flights she eventually found hers and made for the desk.

Checking-in was quick and she was soon sitting in the lounge waiting for the flight to be called.

The Delta flight to West Africa would take eighteen hours, stopping in Paris. She needed to go there to find out about her past but was nervous. She was not a good flyer. The sheer size of the aeroplane, a Boeing 787-8 scared her. It didn't seem so big when she was sitting in the airport lounge waiting to board but getting nearer to it was frightening. By that time, it had grown into the size of a whale. Was this going to be her last trip? She wondered. She thought about it again as she climbed up the shaky stairs and entered.

In fact, the journey was remarkably smooth. She was so relaxed that she slept most of the way and woke up to find they were almost there. A kind gentleman nudged her and whispered, 'I think you need to wake up, we're almost there.'

'Thank you,' she said blushing.

She gathered her belongings together and remembered to put on her shoes. Somewhere she had read that you should always put your shoes on before landing just in case.

Kinshasa, N'djili International Airport was pretty basic; just one terminal reached by a long walk across the tarmac in the blazing sun. Pulling her carry-on luggage, she followed the other passengers as they made their way towards it.

'Passport please,' demanded a female official. Bikita fumbled in her bag and handed it to her.

'How long are you staying?' The officer barked, thumbing through the document.

'Umm, about three or four days.'

'Not more?' she said sounding offended. 'It's a beautiful country.'

'No, it's not that, I'm researching a book and need to get back as soon as possible. I will stay much longer next time and see your wonderful country.'

'Ya, do that,' she said, handing Bikita back her documents.

Chapter Five

Kinshasa Museum

Bikita had booked into the Hotel Hacienda on Avenue De La Justice. She chose it because it was close to the Kinshasa Museum. As she had only been able to set aside a very short time, she didn't want to spend all day travelling. The room was fine and the shower perfect. Standing under it and letting the warm water wash away the dust of the day, Bikita felt excited. She had waited so long for this trip and had planned it in her head many times only to be disappointed when an assignment came in that she needed to deal with.

Later, after a short rest, she was ready to explore. Although the museum was only a short distance from her hotel, it took Bikita almost half an hour to get there, weaving her way through the crowded thoroughfare. The noise was deafening and the air polluted. Everyone in the city must have been out that day, or so it seemed. In her haste, she tripped and almost stepped into a large pothole filled with dirty rainwater. Irritated and frustrated, she finally arrived at the entrance to a modern two-storey building fronted by imitation Portland stone. She climbed the few stairs and entered the large foyer. The air was cool and the sounds of the city were now a distant hum.

The contrast with the outside was striking. She breathed a sigh of relief and stood for a while absorbing the surroundings; Corinthian columns in white marble flanking the main stairway to the first floor. A sign caught her eye, POTTERY. Without thinking she began walking towards the stairs when she heard a man's voice.

'Excuse me, madam.' She turned and saw a uniformed attendant.

'Madam, you will need to buy a ticket,' he said apologetically in a refined English accent.

'Yes of course, I'm sorry. I was so taken with the calm and tranquillity in here compared to outside...' Bikita stuttered.

She followed him to the desk and paid the entrance fee.

'Perhaps you can help me? I have an appointment with your director, Mr Kasonga.'

'What is your name?'

'Trimingham, Ms Bikita Trimingham.'

'You're American?'

'Yes,' she replied, and couldn't resist asking him, 'Your accent? It's British.'

'Yes, I was born in the USA but spent most of my life in London and then returned to my roots ten years ago.'

She glanced at the label on his lapel, David Ademola.

'The director, Mr Kasonga, will be here shortly, you can wait in my office.'

Bikita followed him into a small, brightly lit room. He poured her a glass of water and switched on the AC.

'Excuse me, I need to get on,' he said and left.

The room was sparsely furnished with a table, two chairs and a small bookshelf. Bikita walked over and glanced at the books, mainly English paperbacks. What caught her eye, however, was a book about the British Empire and slavery. She was about to open it when he returned.

'I see you have a book on slavery?'

'Yes, I'm doing a degree at night school; slavery is one of my subjects. Excuse me, Mr Kasonga is here, I will take you to his office.'

Bikita followed him up a flight of stairs to a room off the main corridor. He knocked.

'Come,' a voice from within called out.

They entered.

'Sir, this is Mrs Trimingham. She says she has an appointment to see you.'

'Ah yes, I remember; an American lady rang me.'

He turned to her.

'Good morning Mrs Trimingham, it's a pleasure to meet you.'

Bikita shook his outstretched hand.

'It's Ms, but please call me Bikita.

'How can I help you?'

'First of all, thank you for seeing me. I am very interested in West African pottery. I would like to know more about this piece.'

Handing the shard to him, she continued, 'I found it when I was a child, in my garden, in Georgia in America. I was told that it was typical.'

'Mmm, that's interesting. I think you should show it to our pottery expert, Mr Chukwuemeka. He will know more about it than me. Let me see if he has arrived yet?'

Bikita waited while he dialled his number.

'Hello, good morning, Linet, this is Mr Kasonga, is Mr Chukwuemeka in yet?'

'Yes sir, he has just arrived.'

'Good, tell him I'm sending a visitor, Ms Trimingham from America. She is interested in West African pottery.

Bikita could hear voices.

'He says to send her along.'

It was only a short walk through the galleries to his office. On the way, Bikita saw a wide-ranging display of pottery styles dating back to the 15th century, before colonisation. She was tempted to stop and examine them but she didn't want to keep him waiting. She wanted to learn more about her shard. It had now taken on a life of its own, demanding to be heard and she was impatient to learn about it. She wondered what it would tell her. She had a feeling that it could reveal an amazing adventure that her fore-bearers had experienced.

Bikita was impatient as she knocked on his door.

'Come in.'

Mr Chukwuemeka was much younger than she expected, tall with a shock of black hair.

'Hello Ms Trimingham; welcome. It's nice to put a face to a name.'

'Mr Chukwuemeka, it's a pleasure to meet you.'

'I believe you are interested in West African pottery?'

'Yes, did Mr Kasonga explain to you why I am here?'

'Yes, he said that you had found a shard in the garden at your home in the States.'

'Yes, I was a child at the time. I then lost track of it, but it came to light later when I cleared out my mother's home after she died.'

'Do you have it with you?'

'Yes.'

'May I see it?'

Bikita handed it to him. He studied it for a while turning it over in his hands.

'It's a piece of pottery made in the style of seventeenth-century West Africa.'

She was intrigued. 'How do you know?'

'If you look carefully, you can see parallel lines cut into the surface.'

'Yes, I had noticed those but didn't know what they were.'

'It's a technique called "rouletting." It was widely used in West Africa. The potter takes two or more long pieces of grass or other plant material and winds it together to make a thread. Then using it as an engraving tool, she, usually a woman, impresses the surface of the still soft clay, leaving a series of parallel lines. Using different plants twisted together, a wide range of decorations can be fashioned, each reflecting the taste of the potter. Once air-dried, the pot is placed in a fire until fired. This technique produces low-fired earthenware that is typically hollow, creating bowls and containers that were used for a wide range of purposes such as cooking, serving, and storage of water or grains.

'How do you think it got to America?'

'That's the intriguing part. There are two possible ways. It could have been brought over when slaves were shipped to the USA, or it could have been made in the States by freed, enslaved people. I don't think it is possible to say.'

Bikita thought for a while, trying to imagine how the enslaved would have felt, far away from their homes, from everything familiar, thrown into a foreign country but trying to connect with their old traditions. She felt very sad at the thought. It must have shown on her face because Mr Chukwuemeka interrupted her thoughts.

'Are you okay?'

'Yes, I was imagining what it must have felt like for those unfortunate people.'

Then she had a thought. 'I wonder, is this type of pottery still being made?'

'Yes of course, it is still the pottery of the villages just as it was hundreds of years ago. I don't think the technique has changed much.'

Bikita paused. Could she?

'Would it be possible to visit a village and see the women actually making the pottery and in particular the decoration?'

Chapter Six

Visiting a Village to See Pottery Being Made

Bikita returned to her hotel and waited. She was excited at the prospect of seeing pottery being made locally.

Later that day she got a call. 'Good afternoon, Ms Trimingham.'

It was Mr Kasonga from the museum. She recognised his voice.

'Good afternoon, Mr Kasonga, please call me Bikita.'

'How are you Bikita? Please call me Gabriel.'

'Fine, Gabriel.'

'I have some good news. I have contacted the chief of a local village that still makes traditional pottery and have arranged for you to visit tomorrow morning, if that is convenient?'

'Yes, it's very convenient, that's wonderful.'

Bikita was delighted as she only had another day before she returned home.

'I will pick you up at 10 a.m. from your hotel. Bring a hat and some water. It will be very hot.'

Before she could thank him, he had gone.

The day seemed to pass in a flash and it was suddenly the following morning. Bikita was waiting at the hotel entrance under a parasol loaned to her by the hotel when an old Ford car clattered to a halt. Gabriel peered out of the window.

'Good morning, Bikita. How are you today?'

'Fine, how are you, Gabriel?'

'Good. Hop in and we will be on our way. It's about an hour's drive.'

Jolted and bumped, she sat peering out of the open window as they left the confusion of the city and began to enter the open countryside.

Suddenly a calm descended as they drove along rough marram roads lined by palm trees and passed though small villages consisting of a few straw-made houses with children playing in the yard. After about an hour, they arrived at a larger village in the centre of which was an impressive wooden building with a Makuti roof. No sooner had they parked than they were surrounded by smiling children with their hands outstretched.

'Take no notice,' whispered Gabriel. 'Let's go and meet the chief.'

Bikita followed him between rows of small straw huts until they reached an open square.

'The chief lives in that big house over there,' said Gabriel pointing to a larger building on the edge. 'He is expecting us.'

At that moment, the chief appeared, a tall, heavily built man with a luxuriant white beard. He waved to them and they went over to meet him.

'Welcome,' he roared, proffering his hand.

Bikita shook it. 'Thank you, sir, for kindly arranging to see us.'

'Ms Trimingham, Gabriel tells me that you would like to see our pottery factory?'

'Yes, I would love to see how your ladies make their pots. I found a shard when I was a child and I think it could be related to yours.'

At that moment a slim, lightly tanned young woman appeared. She smiled shyly and curtsied.

'This is my last-born daughter Bethanie. She will take you to the pottery.'

Immediately Bethanie set off and Bikita followed her. After a short walk, they arrived at an open space surrounding a central burnt-out fireplace. Bethanie pointed to the flat open space.

'This is where all our pots are hand-made. We don't have any machinery as some modern potteries do. We fire them in the open over there,' she said pointing to the fireplace.

'Come, let me show you some recently made pots.'

Bikita followed her to where a number of women were seated on the ground with pots on their laps.

'What are they doing?' Bikita asked, bending down to take a closer look.

'They are decorating unfired pots using a traditional method called "rouletting." They take lengths of grasses and stems and wind them together to make a single thread that re-creates their shapes.

She watched speechless as she saw the exact design on her shard being re-created on the still damp earthen pots by these craftswomen. It was a magical moment. She could hardly breathe as tears pricked her eyes.

Seeing her tears, Bethanie asked, 'Are you all right?'

'Yes, I'm fine; just a bit overcome by what I am seeing. It's the exact design that I have here. Look.'

Bikita took out her shard, pale red in colour with a design that was identical with those being made. Bethanie showed it to one of the women.

'*Qu'est-ce que tu penses?*' And in English, 'What do you think this is?'

She studied it for a while turning it over in her hands.

'*Oui. je suis sûr que cela a été fait par un Potière Africain.*' 'Yes, I am sure it was made by an African potter.'

'*Mais je l'ai trouvée en Amérique, comment y est-il arrivé ici?*' 'But I found it in America,' Bikita replied. 'How did it get there?'

Bikita had at last got part of the answer. The design on her shard was West African and possibly Seventeenth or Eighteenth century. Now she needed to find out how it got there. Was it possible that an enslaved African having been forcibly taken to America made it there? That possibility was intriguing.

Chapter Seven

Finding the Husband

The Shard's story actually begins in the sixteenth century, just before the Portuguese invasion of West Africa.

Princess Dalia of Mali had returned from the water hole and was helping her mother cook cassava and rice.

Over the cooking pot, her mother began, 'My dear, your father, the king and I, have been talking about your future.'

Dalia guessed what was coming. They wanted to get her married.

'We think it is time you were married. We have sent out a messenger who has returned with news of a fine husband for you.'

Dalia was not overly excited when she heard the news.

'Mama, it's too soon, I am still a girl. I am not ready for marriage.'

'Nonsense, Dalia, you have seen the red flow and that is a sign that you are ready, so no more nonsense from you. Your father is speaking to the agent and arranging for us to visit.

'But I don't know him. I can't marry a man I have never met.'

'Silence girl, you will marry whom we choose. I hadn't met your father before we married, and it has been very successful.'

'The world is different from your day,' she murmured.

Dalia was downcast. Her friends had just returned from the village and were full of excitement.

'There's a teacher in the village. He wants to arrange lessons for us young people to learn more about the world, the world beyond our village.'

Dalia listened. She often sat looking at the stars and wondered. What was beyond them? Were there other worlds like ours? Why were we here? So many questions. She wanted to learn more.

Chapter Eight

The Preparation

The sun was rising slowly in the East as King Alfonso of Mali, also known as Mvemba a Nzinga, opened his eyes and yawned. His maidservant was instantly awake by his side.

'Bring me water to wash,' he commanded already thinking of the tasks ahead.

The trip to meet Dalia's husband-to-be was not far off and the family needed to organise.

Everyone was excited as the day for the departure approached. The numbers had to be limited and that meant leaving some of the smaller children behind. There were lots of tears when the final list was decided.

'Bring me food and then send for my sons and daughters, I want to discuss the arrangements.'

After a breakfast of porridge and mashed bananas, he made his way to the shade under the Baobab tree to await the family. The word had gone around and slowly his older children arrived.

'*Ututu Oma* — Good Morning, Father' The greeting was echoed by each as they sat down in a circle at his feet.

He began,

'My children, I have called you together to finalise the arrangements for our trip to the Kingdom of Kongo. We are embarking on an exciting but dangerous journey. For it to be successful, we will need to cooperate at every level from the oldest to the youngest. Several days ago, I gave you each a responsibility and would like you to tell us your progress.'

Without waiting, Amare, his eldest son stood up. Short in stature, he had a sturdy build like his father.

'Father, you asked me to plan the trip; to work out a safe route. I have estimated that it will take us three days to reach the Congo river. We will be travelling west towards the setting sun. The weather is changeable at this time of year so we might see some rain. I have arranged for four porters to accompany us to carry our clothes etc. as well as the presents. After crossing the river, we will have another three day's travel until we reach the Kingdom of Kongo.'

'Amare, what presents have you selected?'

'Father, on your advice, I have chosen some gold bracelets, lengths of cloths, decorated pots and various small tokens. I have brought some of them with me for you to see.'

The other members of the family crowded round to admire the items.

'Enough, children, please. We need to concentrate. Thank you, Amare. Razi, tell us your plans for the river crossing.'

Razi was tall and thin, the son of another mother.

'The Congo river is about one thousand paces wide at the crossing. At this time of year, the waters will be high. When we arrive, I will negotiate with the river people who live on its banks for a number of Pirogues — the long narrow boats that they have hewn from trunks of the Tola tree. I think we will need eight but I will see when we get there. At this time of year, the middle of the river is shallower and the current could be fast flowing. We plan to tie the boats together so as not to lose anyone.'

'Good work, Razi. Now Delilah and Keisha, how are you progressing?'

'We are almost complete,' said Delilah, the oldest daughter. 'We have food, salt and water for seven days together with cooking pots and storage jars. We hope to buy fresh fruit and vegetables from local farmers on the way. We will need five servants to carry everything.'

'Finally, Jafera, how are your plans progressing?'

'I am ready Father. We have eight camels prepared, to carry people together with enough goats, chickens and cows in milk to feed us for two weeks.'

'Finally, family, I don't need to remind you of the dangers that await us. We need to be vigilant at all times and protect the children in particular.'

Chapter Nine

Choosing the Wedding Gown

The village was unusually quiet that night. Families were huddled together preparing for the journey, something they had never done before. The children were put to sleep early so as to be rested for the long day ahead.

Dalia was with her mother discussing clothes.

'Mama, I don't know what to wear for the wedding. What do you think?'

'I know you may not agree but why don't you wear my wedding dress? I have kept it hoping that one day it would find a use. I think you will like it.'

After a few minutes, a servant returned with a huge cotton bag. Dalia undid the string, delved into it and removed the dress. It was a full-length gown made of the finest white cotton decorated with overlapping triangles, squares, and circles dyed in many colours.

'Your father, the king, wore a gown made of a similar cloth. Why don't you try it on?'

'May I?'

'Yes of course.'

Dalia returned a few moments later wearing the dress.

'What do you think, Mama?'

'Dear child, it fits you perfectly. What do you think?'

'I love it, may I wear it?'

'Yes of course, you will look beautiful.'

Suddenly there were cries. '*Aidez! Aidez! Un lion.*'

Outside, men were running with sticks towards the pens where the cows had been sheltered for the night. A lioness was trying to break down the barriers. As the men approached, it turned toward them lunging at the nearest one.

'Aaah!' screamed the man as the lioness bit into his leg and started to drag him away.

'*Arretez! Arretez!* Stop! Stop,' the men shouted. Others tried to frighten it away but it just ran off into the dark, the man's screams slowly subsiding. A child's cry could be heard, then silence.

Chapter Ten

Crossing the Congo

The following morning just after sunrise, the party assembled. The camels carrying the families would lead, followed by the carriers loaded high with provisions.

Seated on the leading camel was Amare.

'Leave the sun at your back when we set off,' he shouted, turning to the drivers behind. 'We want to travel west.'

Then came a slow and laborious journey, moving at the rate of the camels. They followed rough paths made by previous generations of animals travelling through the under growth. Occasionally thick vegetation slowed their progress. As the sun rose, thirst and fatigue set in. The older members found camel travel especially uncomfortable and requested regular stops to get down and stretch their legs. Conscious of their difficulty, Amare announced,

'We will rest at noon when the sun is highest and we will make another stop as it gets dark and build a fire on which to cook the evening meal. Then the porters will set about making temporary roofs out of local bushes, and mattresses out of leaves; enough for everyone to have a soft surface to sleep on.'

After the third day, the party arrived on the east bank of the Congo river.

'Look at that? I can't believe it, it's so big.' Gasps of surprise could be heard as no one had ever seen a river, let alone a river of such a size.

Finding a flat area by the riverbank. Amare announced. 'We will camp here.'

As night was falling, a number of the older men assembled to discuss the crossing. Having decided on their plan, they made their way to the nearby village to meet the boatmen. They were met by some local river people.

'Greetings, we are from the east and wish to cross the river to go to the Kingdom of Kongo. Our daughter is marrying the king's son.'

'You are very welcome,' they replied. 'Please sit and drink.' A jug of local wine was passed around.

'How many are you?'

'We are a family, friends and servants, thirty-two people.'

After the details were finalised, it was agreed that eight Pirogues would be needed. The camels would be left behind and cared for by the local people. They would be collected on the return journey.

Later, several women went to the local market to buy fruit paying with Cowrie shells.

The family stayed that night in the village celebrating into the earlier hours. By daybreak, everyone was ready for the crossing. There was a palpable air of excitement as the boats were brought alongside the bank.

'It's going to be fine,' said Delilah to her daughter who was beginning to cry. 'Don't be afraid, we will soon be there.'

After breakfast, the families assembled on the riverbank. The first four boats were loaded, eight people to a boat. The other four boats were filled with the animals and supplies. At a command from Razi, the flotilla of tied boats slowly began to leave the shore. The oarsman, pulling in unison, guided their crafts across the water. As the current caught them, the long line of boats began to meander and zig-zag. When the first boat reached the middle where the water was shallower and flowing faster, it was swept downstream pulling the others with it.

Suddenly there was a shout. All eyes were directed to the last boat which had somehow broken free and was careering out of control. The oarsman was fighting hard to steady it as it bucked and twisted in the spiralling water like a frightened animal. Slowly and patiently, by rowing against the current, he brought it back into line, all the time speaking softly to the occupants.

'Stay calm, I've got it. We will soon be safe.'

Some were fearful and cried out, 'Please be careful, we can't swim.'

From the shore, Razi calmed them, 'It won't be long, you will soon be on dry land.'

'Steady boys,' called the chief oarsman. 'Hold the line.'

41

By rowing hard, the oarsmen slowly realigned the boats settling them back into a straight line. Inch by inch they neared the far shore. As soon as the first boat reached the bank, local men were ready to secure it and to help people get out onto dry land.

As boat by boat was tied up and the occupants stepped ashore, their faces lit up with relief and broad smiles appeared. Once on dry land, the children began to run around, singing and dancing.

As soon as everyone was accounted for, fires were lit and a meal of Chapatti and Sukuma wiki was prepared. The night was spent in the huts of a nearby village, singing and dancing before the journey continued.

Chapter Eleven

Preparing for the Wedding

The Kingdom of Kongo was agog with excitement at the coming wedding. It was on everyone's lips.

'Have you heard? The bride is only two days away? She is beautiful and comes with gifts of gold.'

Scouts had returned to say that they had seen a long column of camels bringing the family from the east and had spoken to them.

'We bring greetings from the King of Kongo, who are you?'

'Greetings to you and your kingdom. We are from the Kingdom of Mali east of the Congo river. We are bringing Princess Dalia, a bride to marry the King of Kongo's son.

'You are welcome,' replied the scouts. 'We will go ahead and let them know that you are on the way.'

At the palace, everyone was busy preparing for the big day. The scouts had reported to the king that they had met the bride's family

'Your highness, the princess and her family are expected to arrive in two days.'

The king thanked them. 'Good we will be ready to receive them.'

Chapter Twelve

Meeting the King of Kongo and his Family

The sun was high in the clear sky when the first of the bride's party arrived in the Kingdom of Kongo. Soon the village square was resounding with welcoming conversations as old friends re-connected, often not having seen each other for years.

Suddenly there was a round of drums. Everyone went quiet as the king wearing his golden gown emerged from his hut. Walking slowly to the middle of the square, he began, 'My dear friends, welcome to my kingdom. Please join us,' he said spreading out his arms.

Tables and stools had been set out in the shade of the trees and a wide range of hot and cold food had been laid out. There was a crush as the hungry visitors rushed forwards and helped themselves. They sat down and began eating.

'I hope we've put out enough food, they're a hungry lot,' he whispered to his wife. She smiled. He was always on the stingy side.

'We can always get more if we need to,' she whispered.

Chapter Thirteen

Thwarted

Abioye looked on, searching the crowd for a glimpse of his wife to be but she was nowhere in sight.

'Come,' he whispered to his brother, Chikae. 'Let's go and find her.'

'No! You know what Mother said; you are not to see her before the wedding.'

'C'mon, I can't wait until then. Are you coming?'

The two young men slowly backed away from the crowd and slipped behind some bushes. They waited until the party was in full swing hoping that no one would notice their absence and then made their way towards the women's huts.

The king, who was in conversation with one of the visiting leaders, saw a movement behind a bush. He turned and spotted his two sons disappearing behind the huts. He realised immediately what they were up to and acted.

'Guards! Quick, it's my sons; follow them and stop them before they reach the women's huts.'

The two young men continued, unaware that they were being followed. They crouched down low whenever anyone was passing by. They had almost reached the woman's hut when they were confronted by two burly guards who pinned their arms to their sides.

'Come on, Abioye, sir,' the taller said, 'this is no place for you. Let's go back to the party.'

'Why?' He retorted angrily. 'Get out of my way, we were just getting some fresh air.'

'I know,' the guard said patiently, taking him firmly by the arm. 'Let's just walk back quietly please sir.'

On the way back, Chikae whispered,

'I am afraid, Abioye, you are just going to have to wait and hope she is beautiful.'

Dalia was washing her hair when she heard loud voices outside her hut. Covering her face, she peered out and saw the guards having a heated conversation with two young men. Puzzled at first, it slowly dawned on her that one of them must be her husband-to-be, but which one?

'Mama,' she whispered, 'I think I have just seen my husband-to-be.'

'That's impossible. You mustn't see him until the wedding, that is our tradition.'

'But that's so old-fashioned.'

'Maybe, but it's our way and you must obey it.'

Dalia couldn't sleep. She tossed and turned, repeatedly seeing the young men's faces. Which one will be my husband? she wondered, and the question kept tormenting her. Did it matter? She finally decided it didn't, and slept.

Chapter Fourteen

Second Thoughts

Dalia woke with a start. Suddenly she remembered. Today was her marriage day. It was going to change her life forever. Dread engulfed her. What am I going to do? She wanted to flee, to go back home and join her friends and forget about marriage but she knew it was too late.

Her thoughts were suddenly interrupted.

'Get up. Dalia, it's late. We have a lot to do,' shouted her mother pulling back the drapes. The bright sun lit up the room and momentarily blinded her.

'Mama, I don't want to get married. I'm too young,' she pleaded, tears pouring down her cheeks.

'Nonsense child, we have been over all this before. Now get up and go to the stream and wash.'

Dalia returned to find her mother laying out some clothes.

'What are you doing, Mama?'

'I am putting out your bridal gown.'

Laid out on the matting floor was the white cotton dress worn by her mother. Dalia touched it letting her thoughts linger. She would wear it with pride. Although she had originally wanted to make her own choice now that the wedding was almost upon her, she felt the weight of history and realised that her mother was right to insist.

'I am so honoured to be wearing your dress,' she said, hugging her.

'Thank you, dear. You have made me very happy. You will look beautiful. He is a very lucky man.'

'But he doesn't know me.'

'Hush child, he will fall in love with you immediately he sees you, just like your father did when he saw me.'

Dalia watched as her mother went to a small box and took out an object. She unwrapped it and handed it to her.

'Dalia, this is something I want to give you, a keepsake. It's been in our family for longer that I can remember.'

At first Dalia didn't know what it was and then as she turned it over in her hands, she realised it was a piece of broken pottery.

'Mama, what is it for?'

'Darling it is very precious. It is part of a bowl that your great grandmother made as a wedding present to my mother. We were several children and because she wanted each of us to have part of it, she broke it into pieces and gave each of her children a piece. So, I am giving you my piece to cherish as a reminder of the noble family from which you have come.'

In another part of the village, the groom was unhappy. He was getting prepared in ceremonial dress.

'Father, it's outrageous; anyone would think we were living in the fifteenth century. Just because you married my mother without seeing her, doesn't mean that I have to do the same. I have a good mind to leave and just run away.'

'Come on, Abioye, don't be a fool. One day you will inherit my kingdom. Be patient and follow tradition. Once you are married, you can play around a bit as I did.'

The king handed him a long golden-coloured gown with a tiger-skin belt around the waist.

'Try this on, I wore it for my wedding.'

Abioye made a face but put it on. It fitted perfectly.

'And let me put this on you, my father gave it to me.'

The king leaned forwards and hung a heavy golden chain around his son's neck. Finally, he placed a crown adorned with flamingo feathers on the boy's head.

'That will do. Now you look like a king's son. She will love you at first sight.'

Chapter Fifteen

The Wedding

The wedding ceremony was to be held at midday in the huge village square. The space could seat up to two hundred people. Workers had already put into place two thrones at one end. A flowered arch had been constructed under which the ceremony would be conducted.

The morning looked like rain with dark billowy clouds but by the afternoon the sky had cleared. Excitement was in the air. The two families had assembled and were seated on the ground on either side of an aisle at the head of which were the two thrones. Suddenly a loud drumming was heard and two rows of dancers appeared, women in front and men behind.

'Look Mama,' whispered a small girl, 'It's our sister, she is in the front row.' The dancer's rhythm increased into a frenzy and then it suddenly stopped.

King Henrique of Kongo stood up and raised his arms. The crowd quietened.

'Friends, it is my great honour to welcome you to the wedding of my son, Abioye, to Princess Dalia, the daughter of our neighbour, the King of Mali. It will recognise the joining of our two great kingdoms ensuring continued peaceful coexistence.'

Many present still remembered the bloody violence that had erupted between the two kingdoms several years earlier. Onlookers gasped as Abioye, dressed in traditional vestments appeared, He stood for a moment smiling at the crowd and then walked slowly towards the flowered arch. On reaching it, he turned and stood under it on the right-hand side looking back into the crowd. A roll of drums introduced the bride. She entered accompanied by her mother. Dressed in the fine white cotton gown dyed in many colours, her head and face were concealed by a veil. She was accompanied by cheers and loud clapping.

Halfway down the aisle, her mother stepped to the side leaving Dalia alone in the aisle. She continued advancing slowly between the two groups of onlookers until she stopped opposite the groom. The two were facing each other for the first time. Abioye peered forwards, trying to see through Dalia's veil.

Dalia's inner thoughts:

'He looks rather handsome, maybe this won't be so bad, Mama could be right.'

Abioye's inner thoughts:

'I'll know what she looks like soon enough and there'll be nothing I can do about it.'

The priest, a man in his sixties with a luxuriant black beard stepped forwards and faced the couple. Before him was a wooden table on which he had placed four small bowls, each containing a different substance: lemon, vinegar, cayenne pepper and honey.

'Please remove the bride's veil,' he said to her mother who was now standing nearby.

There was a gasp from the crowd with clapping and shouts of 'Bravo!' as they saw the bride's face for the first time.

The priest continued. 'Dalia and Abioye, in front of you, are four bowls. They contain lemon for sourness, vinegar for bitterness, cayenne pepper for hotness and honey for sweetness. They are a reminder that the journey you are embarking upon together, will be a mixture of happiness and sadness.'

The two leaned forwards over the bowls and together tasted their contents.

'Ughh,' whispered Dalia as she sampled the pepper.

The marriage ceremony itself was very quick. The two agreed to love, cherish, protect and support each other. And before they could settle their nerves, Abioye and Dalia were married and walking back through the cheering crowds, hand in hand.

'You are very beautiful,' Abioye whispered in Dalia's ear.

'And you are very handsome,' added Dalia.

When on their own, Dalia would later tell Abioye that she had felt her heart thumping in her chest, and that she had never been so alone and so scared.

Chapter Sixteen

The Honeymoon

Later that day as the celebrations were beginning to quieten and the two of them were alone in the marriage hut, Abioye whispered to Dalia. 'Dalia, dearest, let's go somewhere quiet. I want to tell you about my plans for our honeymoon.'

'Honeymoon? What's that?'

'It has become usual for newly wedded couples to go away on their own after the wedding to get to know each other.'

Dalia looked surprised. 'I don't know that my mother will agree, she wants me to go to the married women's house so that they can teach me.'

'Your mother is so old-fashioned. Let me teach you, it would be fun. There's a hut by the banks of Lake Tumba. It's about a day's journey away. We would be on our own away from the prying eyes of our parents. What do you think?'

It took longer than they expected but after a two-day trek, they arrived at the banks of the lake, a large oval shaped basin of fresh water. Dalia saw it first.

'Abioye, look! I can see the lake.'

'Where?

'See? Through the trees, over to the right. The water is gleaming in the sunlight.'

'Yes, that's it. I think the hut is just around that corner. Follow me, but be careful the rocks are a bit uneven. Here, give me your hand.'

As they walked further, the bushes separated and the full extent of the lake could be seen. Suddenly a fish jumped, breaking the glassy surface of the water and falling back with a splash which echoed in the stillness. In the distance, snow-capped mountains rose up, silhouetted against the blue sky.

'It's beautiful here, like paradise. Thank you for bringing me.'

'Come let's go into the water.'

'I can't swim.'

'Come, don't be afraid, we won't go far.'

Abioye began to take off his clothes. He nodded to Dalia.

She blushed. 'I have never taken my clothes off in front of a man,' she whispered.

'I won't look,' he laughed walking slowly into the water.

She watched him, admiring his broad shoulders and narrow hips. Then shrugging her shoulders, she undressed. It was a strange feeling, standing there without clothes. It felt free and natural, not at all embarrassing. He turned and put out his hand, encouraging her to join him.

'Come, the water is beautiful and refreshing.'

She stepped in carefully, her feet sinking into the soft sand. As she came near to him, she couldn't resist splashing some water on his back.

'Oooh,' he cried, laughing and turning to splash her. Soon they were in a splashing frenzy. Exhausted and with water dripping from their bare bodies, they clung to each other. It was the first time she had ever touched a man.

The days flashed by; an early morning dip; breakfast of mandazi and milk; a walk and then lunch of fish caught that morning. Later a rest and their first tentative lovemaking. It seemed to them both that life couldn't get any better.

Chapter Seventeen

The Attack

It would be years later that Dalia, now a grandmother would be able to tell the story of her enslavement.

'What happened, Grandma?' asked her youngest grandchild, a small boy with dark, frizzy hair.

'Your grandfather and I had only been married for a few weeks when we decided to have a honeymoon.

'A honeymoon, what's that, Grandma?'

'It's a sort of a holiday that a newly married couple have to go on, to get to know each other. You spend some time together on our own.'

'Didn't you know each other before you got married?'

'In those days, our parents arranged whom we were to marry, not like today. After the wedding, we had travelled to a nearby lake and were staying in a small straw house on the outskirts of a village. One night we were woken by shouts and banging. I shook your grandfather...'

'Abioye, go and see what the commotion is about. I expect it's some local village boys having fun.'

He got up grumbling about being disturbed and went to the door and peeked out. He came back, his face drawn.

'What is it?' I asked.

'Some strange men, I didn't recognise them. They are carrying sticks and are shouting and breaking everything.'

Then it happened...

'What happened?' The children shouted together.

'The men broke into our hut and grabbed us and tied our arms behind our backs. Grandpa tried to stop them but they hit him over the head. It was awful and I was very frightened.'

'What happened then?' the children asked in unison.

'We were marched to the edge of the village where a number of other men and women whom we didn't know were tied up. We didn't recognise our captors, who were from a faraway village...'

'Let us go immediately,' Abioye commanded. 'My father, the King of Kongo will send out a search party and you will all be punished.'

'Shut up, you may call yourself the son of a king but to us you are property to be sold.'

'Sold? What do you mean, sold?'

'As slaves!'

That was the first time we had heard about the trade in human beings.

'You won't get away with this,' Abioye shouted but before he could continue, he was hit and fell to the ground.'

'At least let us stay together,' he begged.

'No! men and women are to be separated.'

Chapter Eighteen

Abioye's Story

My heart dropped as I saw Dalia being tied up and taken away. She looked back and mouthed 'I love you.' I feared I would never see her again.

The following days and weeks passed in a nightmare of fear, pain and hunger. Tied together in a line of other prisoners, I dragged myself along. We passed by small villages and through dense forests, travelling at night to avoid detection. Days and nights merged and I lost track of time. After what seemed like ages, we reached the seashore and were bundled into a stark, prison-like building. At least we could rest I thought, not prepared for what was to come. Each of us was branded with our owner's initials burned into our flesh. Then we were shackled to a wall with minimal space between us. Every day, we were unshackled and marched along a corridor out onto the beach where we could wash and defecate. Then back to the hell hole. There was little conversation but what I heard frightened me. Some men said that ships would dock and take on board hundreds of us, to be shipped abroad. Where and for what, I did not know. And where was Dalia? I missed her greatly and feared that she was dead.

Chapter Nineteen

Dalia's Story

I couldn't believe what was happening when they dragged Abioye away shouting and struggling. He was no match for them and suddenly he was gone. I was alone with the other women. Then followed a nightmare. Days merged into nights as we were herded along. I lost track of time but it must have been many days later before we stopped in front of a large, grim-looking building. We were then forced into a large room and each chained to a wall. I thought we were near the sea as I could hear waves crashing on the shore and seagulls cawing. When it was quiet, I could hear the cries of men being beaten somewhere else in the building. Chained near me was a young woman, close enough so that we could speak in a whisper.

'What do they call you?' I asked.

She didn't move at first. The light was poor and I thought that she could be dead.

'What are you called?' I repeated.

I saw her open her eyes.

'Efemena,'

'Where are you from?'

'Me come from the Omo tribe of Benin.'

'How you get here?' I whispered hoping no guards would hear me.

'It so sudden. Me in field walking home when dem men grab me. Me screamed but not heard. Why we here? Me scared.'

'I don't know. You be brave. We stay together.' She smiled.

The next day I learned our fate. Someone whispered to me, 'They take us away, across the water.'

Chapter Twenty

The Middle Passage

The crossing from Africa to the Americas was later to be referred to as 'The Middle Passage.' It was the journey taken by enslaved men and women from West Africa to America and the West Indies. Although originally established by the Portuguese, British merchants very soon got wind of it and began to ply the same route. Old schooners were quickly refitted so as to accommodate hundreds of slaves in their lower decks.

Up to five hundred souls were transported on each journey of about six weeks from the West coast of Africa to the Americas. Their conditions were atrocious. They were kept in crowded conditions, chained for most of the day. Up to ten percent died on the way and their bodies thrown overboard.

As the news of this 'trade' leaked out, more and more pressure was applied, to make it illegal. The state of Georgia was one of the first American states to do so, and between 1735-50 it proposed a ban, but as the value of rice increased and with the difficulty in employing white labourers in its cultivation, pressure was applied to resume the slave trade. Wealthy landowners such as James Oglethorpe the Earl of Egmont opposed its abolition on social and economic grounds. Eventually the House of Commons relented and in 1851, Georgia reinstated slavery after having banned it for over a century.

The last schooner to ply The Middle Passage was the *Wanderer*. Built in 1857 as a luxury sailing vessel, it was sold a year later and converted into a slave ship. Sailing under the flag of the New York Yacht Club, it arrived at the mouth of the Congo and easily evaded the patrols of the British African Squadron. On September 16th, 1858, it sailed up the Congo, docked and took on board about five hundred Africans, imprisoned in the slave warehouses. The owners paid the slavers the equivalent of $50 a head in rum, gunpowder and weapons, and on October 18th, 1858, after less than a month, it began its six weeks return journey during which a hundred people died on the voyage.

Both Dalia and Abioye were on its last voyage. Dalia was with other women imprisoned at the stern, away from the men. The conditions were cramped and unhygienic. Several babies were born during the six weeks but few survived the heat, and the lack of food and water for their mothers.

Chapter Twenty-one
Journey at Sea

Abioye's Story

One day, I woke to find the guards were very busy. The word went around that a ship had docked and that we would be loaded on board.

'Get up,' shouted the guard prodding me with a stick.

'You are going for a sailing trip,' he smirked, 'to get some fresh air.'

We were lined up, prodded and beaten as we dragged ourselves across the landing onto the ship. We were stripped of our clothing. The smell of faeces and sweat made me retch but I would get used to it. Pushed and prodded, we were forced down some steps into a lower deck. Then we were compelled to lie down, side-by-side in the hold of the ship and shackled to the wall. I lost count of how many were loaded but it was many hundreds. It was later that day that I heard the rattle of the rigging and the hiss of the sails. Then the hull beneath me began to roll as we set off. Soon the air became foetid as so many were compressed together,

'We need air,' I shouted but no one came. I managed to turn towards the hull where I could feel cool air coming in and soon feel asleep.

Once out at sea, we soon got into a routine. In the good weather, we were brought onto the deck and allowed to wash and to exercise. Many were seasick which added to their discomfort. Luckily, I have a good stomach and provided I kept away from the smell, I was okay. Unknown to me, Dalia was imprisoned in another part of the same ship.

Days passed into weeks as we ploughed our way through the sea. Surprisingly, I began to like the slow roll of the ship although many hated it as they fought against seasickness.

Dalia's Story

I was in a line of women. We were tied together. No one knew where we were going. It seemed that we would never be allowed to rest. Some women stumbled and fell. We tried to stop and help them but they whipped us and we had to leave them. We seemed to be walking forever but then we smelled the sea and were allowed to rest locked up in a stone house by the coast. We had little food and many of the older women died. The slavers let us bury them but shoved and prodded us when we tried to say a short prayer like the missionaries had taught us.

I was shocked when I saw the ship, it seemed as big as a mountain. Then I became really frightened as they began to force us onto it. I could hear men's voices but didn't know where they were coming from. We were pushed into low-ceilinged spaces with little light and were chained to the walls. I saw terrible things; women raped; women whipped until their backs were pouring blood, then left unconscious on the deck with birds pecking at their dried blood. Few survived such brutality. The dead were flung overboard.

From my occasional time on deck and with a clear sky, I could see a very bright star which I knew meant we were travelling west. No one knew what lay ahead, or what country we were bound for.

Chapter Twenty-two

Enslaved in Georgia

On November 28th 1858, almost fifty years after slavery had originally been banned, four hundred and nine slaves were put ashore on Georgia's Jekyll Island and then shipped to illegal domestic markets in Savannah, Augusta, South Carolina and Florida.

Suddenly everything changed. The ship had stopped moving. Voices could be heard shouting orders. Abioye wondered what was going on and then realised that they must have arrived somewhere, but where? He heard the name Jekyll Island and nudged his neighbour bound next to him.

'Did you hear that? Jekyll Island, where is that?'

'I don't know, it could be anywhere, let's wait and see.'

Then everything seemed to happen. Guards rushed in and began shouting. 'Up; move; we've arrived and you are getting out.'

They undid the chains attaching them to the walls and re-chained the men in a long line. Slowly they dragged themselves upright. Pulled and jolted, they filed out onto the top deck and into the fresh air.

It was the first sight of land they had seen for ages. They had been at sea for six weeks. But what was going to happen now? Abioye knew he must get free, but how?

He found himself in a long line of prisoners being herded off the ship and onto the shore. Then with shouts and whips, they were forced into a large barn-like structure. There the chains joining them were unlocked and they were re-attached to the barn walls as they were in the ship. No one could move more than a few feet before the chains restrained him. Escape seemed impossible and Abioye resigned himself to the situation.

He later learned that by 1800, Henry DuBignon Jr. had become the owner of Jekyll Island, having inherited it from his father, Joseph DuBignon. He had arranged the landing of *Wanderer* and planned to dispatch all the enslaved to the slave markets in South Carolina and Florida.

Chapter Twenty-three

The Underground Railroad

Somewhere in the distance, Dalia could hear a song. A slow sad female voice was singing, 'Swing low, sweet Chariot, coming for to carry me home.' To Dalia, home seemed a long, long way away. Would she ever see it again?

Then, 'Shush,' a voice in the dark. 'Don't speak. I'm a friend.'

Dalia went cold, who could this be? Alone and desperate, who could be a friend?

'Don't be afraid — we are here to help you get away.' A warm hand rested on her shoulder guiding her in the pitch dark. 'It's not far now.'

Dalia saw a door open and lights in a passageway. She followed the stranger down the corridor into a small, poorly lit kitchen. Some stew was cooking on the grate. A plate was handed to her.

'Help yourself.'

'Thank you, I'm starving,' she whispered and then, 'Who are you?'

A pause. 'We don't have names just numbers. I'm twenty-seven.'

'You look younger.'

'No, it's not my age — we need to remain anonymous in case we are...' her voice tried off.

'I understand,' mumbled Dalia fighting to keep her eyes open.

'Look, there's a couch over there. Why don't you lie down, you look exhausted. We won't be leaving until later.'

No sooner had her head hit the pillow than Dalia was asleep. Almost immediately the dream reappeared. The same one she had had almost every night, such that she dreaded closing her eyes. A man was calling to her from the sea.

'Help!' She could just see him and leaned over to try and help him. She recognised his face, it was Abioye but she couldn't reach him. Desperately she stretched out, almost falling in herself. She saw his face pleading and then he slowly disappeared beneath the waves.

Suddenly she was awake. The room was unfamiliar. Confused, she tried to get up and banged into a table. A voice came from the dark, 'It's okay, you're safe. Go back to sleep, we have a long journey tomorrow.'

'Where are you taking me?'

'To freedom. Trust me.'

The following day, Dalia met other escapees; bedraggled and exhausted; young mothers carrying small babies and older men, scarred and branded. No one spoke, each was locked in his own fear and pain, uncertain of the future. Each was conscious that at any moment, a bounty hunter, usually a white man, but occasionally a black man, would appear and drag them back to be flayed and returned to their masters.

The days merged into nights. The group, seven in all, moved slowly from house to house, sleeping in the day and travelling at night. She learned that many of them had been enslaved for years, working in the cotton fields. Most were emaciated and weak from prolonged starvation. As she travelled north and went from refuge to refuge, she saw how the countryside changed. Wide open prairies were replaced by dense forests. The warm weather was giving way to colder and the days were becoming shorter. She heard names like Savannah, Charleston, Virginia and many more; places that they had passed through in the dark.

'We are heading north for Buffalo and the Niagara river,' someone whispered. 'Once we cross it, we will be free.'

The word 'free' sounded so good to Dalia. She had almost given up hope of ever being free. In the quiet of the night, she yearned to be back in her own country with Abioye. They had had so little time together before it happened. The thought of freedom confused her.

'I can't ever be free without Abioye,' she sobbed.

Some five miles ahead, another group, of men, including Abioye, was making their way towards Canada and freedom. He dreamed of Dalia every night not knowing whether she was still alive. Tired of travelling and feeling weary and despondent, he asked one of the guides where they were headed.

'We are going towards the Niagara river. It has become a favourite crossing spot.'

'Why there?'

'Because we have friends there. Many hotels have been built for the tourists who come to marvel at the falls. Most are staffed with African waiters and bellboys, many of whom have escaped slavery, so we have a number of friends who will help us if need be. You can relax, you'll soon be free.'

Abioye felt a surge of hope, but without Dalia, would life have any meaning?

Later that day, having arrived at the Niagara river, he was in a small group of escapees waiting to board the boat to cross. They were to be joined by another group. He was sitting in the shade under a tree when the second group, mainly women, arrived.

In a distraught state, their clothes in shreds, they were exhausted, the younger women helping the older ones. Scanning their lined and grimy faces, Abioye thought he saw someone familiar. Despite her fatigue and filthy condition, he recognised Dalia, her face older and strained.

'Dalia,' he shouted, 'Dalia!' She looked up, surprised and confused. Was someone calling her name? Then she heard it again. A man was running towards her, waving his arms and shouting her name.

'Dalia, Dalia it's me!' Then she recognised him. It was Abioye. Her heart jumped in her chest and then they were in each other's arms, crying and laughing. Briefly forgetting their own fatigue, the other women crowded round them cheering and wanting to share their joy.

'Hurry, we haven't got much time,' said the ship's captain. 'We need to set sail before sundown. I can only take thirty people at a time. But we should have enough time for two trips today.'

Once on board, Dalia and Abioye couldn't stop hugging each other. Between crying and laughing, they pieced together their journey.

'So, we were both on the same ship!' exclaimed Dalia, tears of joy running down her face. 'I didn't know, I thought you were dead.'

Chapter Twenty-four

Safe in Canada

It seemed unreal to Dalia and Abioye that they were at last free. But their long separation and the memory of the journey had left its mark. They felt like strangers. Whenever Abioye reached out to kiss her, Dalia recoiled. He wanted to continue from where they had left off, but it was not the same for Dalia. What she had seen and experienced had left deep scars.

'I can't, Abioye. Please give me time. I need to regain my confidence. It was a terrible experience. I can never forget what I have seen and gone through. Human beings treated worse than animals, women defiled and humiliated; made to do things that no one should be required to do. You will never understand.'

'Dearest Dalia, I love you and will do anything to help you to get out of the place you are in.' Abioye decided to say nothing about his own experiences. He had seen men beaten till the skin on their backs was flayed and running with rivers of blood. Injured men thrown overboard calling out to be saved with no one allowed to help them as they sank, struggling, beneath the waves.

'I can't believe we are here, free!' Dalia kept saying to herself. It seemed so improbable when she was a prisoner and yet now she could go where she wanted. Freedom was so strange — you could do what you want; no one controlling you; no one reducing you to an object, to be cast aside at will.

'Abioye,' she would repeatedly call out, laughing, 'we are free!' And he would rush to her side and they would hug.

'Yes dear. We are free.'

'Let's go out,' she would say.

'Where to?'

'Anywhere, just out. I want to practice this new freedom — to learn what it really is. To have as much of it as possible in case it is taken away from us again. I couldn't bear that,' she would say, her face creasing in pain.

'Darling it's not going to happen. Never again. Try to forget the past. Look to the future. We have our whole lives ahead.'

Chapter Twenty-five

Enlisting

The Civil War between the Union and the Confederates was fought from 1861-1865.

'Dalia, I have just heard that a war is brewing.'

'War! We have had enough of war, I just want some peace.'

'You don't understand; the southern states have joined together in violation of the constitution to form a confederacy.'

'What's that got to do with us? Let them get on with it.'

'Dearest Dalia, it's not as simple as that. I want to help.'

'Help? What can you do?'

'I can fight to stop slavery so that no one has to go through what we did, ever again. It's complicated but basically the south wants to protect their right to have slaves, contrary to the Law of Emancipation signed by Abraham Lincoln.'

'What was that?'

'The Emancipation Proclamation held that all persons held as slaves shall be forever free.'

'That's wonderful! But we are free, no longer walking in fear, our children will grow up as free citizens.'

'That's fine as long as we stay here in the north, but what if we want to go south where it's warmer and where more of our people live?'

'So, what do you want to do?'

'I want to enlist.'

Dalia's heart sank at the word 'enlist.' They had gone through so much.

A few days later, Abioye presented himself at the recruitment office. The room was crowded with fellow African-Americans, wanting to enlist.

Finally, he reached the head of the queue. An officer was seated at a desk filling in application forms.

'Name?'

'Abioye.'

'Abioye what?

'Abioye Kongo.'

'Place of birth?'

'Kingdom of Kongo.'

'Where's that?

'Okay, just put River Road, Niagara, Canada.'

'Skills?'

'Farming.'

'Anything else?'

Abioye thought for a moment. He wanted to be a soldier.

'Yes, hunting and shooting. I want to fight.'

The officer was confused. Because of prejudice against them, he had been told to place African-American volunteers in non-combat support functions.

'Okay, you want to fight? I will do what I can.'

Chapter Twenty-six

The Battle of Antietam

15th September 1862
My Dear Dalia,

I hope this brief note finds you well. The farm must be yielding well now that the rain has come. I am sorry not to write sooner but I have been in training, learning to use the weapons needed to win this war.

We have the most modern guns, repeating firearms that don't need re-loading. I am in the 54th Massachusetts regiment — it's all African and makes me feel at home with my fellow countrymen.

Sorry, have just been called to parade and must close.

I think of you every day and pray that we will be together very soon.

Your loving husband,
Abioye

19 September 1862
My Dear Dalia

I hope you are well. I am in the hospital. Please don't worry, I have a minor leg wound and should be recovered very soon. The good news is we have just won a mighty battle that may turn the tide to end the war in our favour. We faced the Confederate army at Antietam Creek near Sharpsburg in Maryland. Under the command of Major General George McLennan, we attacked the Confederate forces along the creek. I was in the second assault. Together we advanced with our guns blazing. It was a bloody affair; men were dropping all around me.

Then I received a musket in my leg and fell. I lay on the ground for some hours until the First Aid arrived and took me to a field hospital nearby. The doctor says I should be back to the front very soon.

I count the days until we will be together again
Your loving husband,
Abioye

26th September 1862
My Dear Dalia,

Please be brave. I have had to have my right leg removed below the knee. The musket wound became gangrenous, and I became very ill. Happily, I am now on the mend. I should be home soon.

Dalia felt her heart stop.

'Oh my God,' she exclaimed, feeling faint. He's lost a leg. How will we manage?'

Then she felt a sudden surge of strength and a small voice inside her said, 'Yes, we will manage. I will be his other leg and together we will succeed.'

She read on:

I expect to be medically retired soon,
Your Loving Husband,
Abioye

Some weeks later, Dalia was in the garden weeding, when she saw someone far away, waving frantically.

'Dalia, Dalia,' she heard her name being called but didn't recognise him at first. Then it was Abioye, thinner and older, but him.

Dropping the hoe she rushed towards him, shouting, 'Abioye, Abioye, it's you!'

Then they were in each other's arms, laughing and crying.

Taking his bag, she walked with him to the house.

'Sit down. what can I get you?'

'Just some water please.'

He looked so tired and strained, she thought as she carried the jug of water to him. But she was not prepared for what she was to see. While she was in the kitchen, he had removed his artificial leg and rested his stump on a cushion.

'Oh,' she screamed, completely overcome by its appearance. The leg below the knee was missing. The short stump that remained looked like a rounded ball of flesh.

Dalia recoiled from it.

'Don't be afraid, you can touch it. It won't hurt me.'

Gradually Dalia got used to it and when they were on their own she would gently massage it. In time, Abioye was fitted with a new artificial leg that enabled him to walk almost as normal.

Chapter Twenty-seven

Returning to Georgia

Returning to Georgia was confusing. They had both changed; no longer the carefree couple that they were. What were they going to do? They had nothing and the future looked grim, but help was at hand. Thanks to the Refugee Home Society, they were soon the proud owners of a small homestead with twenty acres of land at the Puce River settlement. There the peace and quiet of the farm allowed them to begin the process of healing.

Every morning Abioye would leap out of bed and grab Dalia.

'Come, dear, look.'

Together they would admire the view. Their small patch of land was beginning to grow potatoes, carrots and cabbages. Beyond was a forest, with its huge tree trunks reaching into the sky, and in the distance they could see white-capped mountains.

One morning, Dalia was awakened by a shout.

'Come Dalia, look what I have grown.'

Sleepy-eyed, Dalia came to the back door and looked out. Abioye was standing with both hands full of what looked like brown balls.

'Abioye, what are they?'

'They're called potatoes, a bit like our yams or sweet potatoes but they're white inside.'

'How do you eat them?'

'My neighbour told me to scrub the soil off them. You don't have to remove the skin, just boil them. Let's try some for lunch.'

Sitting together and eating lunch, Abioye could see that Dalia was much more at ease, her shakiness had disappeared and she was putting on weight.

'Dearest, you look beautiful, just like your old self. How do you feel?'

She blushed.

'I am doing fine. I have lost that feeling of fear that anyone coming near was going to take me away. My body has returned to normal and I think I am ready to have a baby.'

Abioye wondered if they would ever see their country again, see their parents, brothers and sisters. Was this country going to be their country? The thought brought sadness.

Dalia saw his face darken.

'What is it dear, what is troubling you? Why are you looking so sad?'

'I was thinking of our home across the water. Will we ever see our families again?'

She got up and put her arms around him.

'Dearest Abioye. God has spared us and blessed us to live in safety. We must not look back but be grateful. Our families will always be in our thoughts, no matter how far away they are.'

Chapter Twenty-eight

Sometime Later

'Dalia are you at home?' Abioye called, letting himself into the house. 'I have some amazing news.'

'I'm upstairs in the bedroom. I'll be down in a few minutes.'

Abioye couldn't wait. 'I'm coming up.'

He bounded upstairs and rushed into the room.

'Why are you so excited?' Dalai asked looking up from finishing making the bed.

'I have just heard some wonderful news. They are repatriating people to Africa. We can go home.'

'Home! How do you mean, home?'

'An organisation called The American Colonization Society is helping to resettle enslaved Africans in their home countries. I went to see them. It's amazing news. They will help us to go home.'

Abioye stopped. Something was wrong. Dalia's face furrowed. The smile had gone.

'What is it, Dalia? Aren't you excited at the chance of going home to be with our families?'

'Yes of course I'm excited. I want to see them, but...'

'But, what?'

'I don't know. I'm scared. We have made a home here, we are safe. I like it here.'

'So, do I but it's not our country, we will always be strangers. We can hardly speak the language.'

Dalia began to smile.

'Dearest, I've been waiting to tell you.'

'Tell me what?'

'I'm pregnant.'

'Pregnant?'

Abioye couldn't believe what she was saying. They had been trying for so long that he had almost given up hope that it would ever happen.

'Darling, are you sure?'

'Yes, I have had no show for over three months.'

'That's wonderful, I'm so happy. Sit down, you must rest, let me help you.'

Laughing, Dalia replied, 'It's okay. I feel fine, don't fuss over me. I'll let you know when I need help. Now go back and finish the garden hut. You promised it would be finished last week.'

'You're right, I'll get on with it. You be careful.'

Resting for a while after doing some heavy lifting, Abioye thought about the conversation they had just had. Maybe she's right? He had always assumed that they would go home if they ever became free. but now, with the baby on the way? Perhaps they should wait until it was born and then decide. Shaking his head, he returned to repairing the hut.

Chapter Twenty-nine

Dalia is Pregnant

Abioye was suddenly awake. He heard Dalia in the kitchen shouting,

'Come quickly, I felt the baby kick,' she called out. 'Our baby kicked me. Abioye, come. Feel my belly.'

'Coming,' he called, jumping out of bed.

Dalia was sitting in a chair.

'Put your hand on my stomach.'

Abioye tentatively pressed on her stomach.

'Can you feel anything?'

'No, what should I feel?'

'Harder, you have to press harder. What can you feel now?'

'Just a firmness.'

'Wait…'

'Wow! yes, I felt something hard then it was gone.'

'That's it. Our baby has just kicked you.'

The long summer days shortened as winter approached. Dalia was counting the time to the birth but her thoughts were filled with sadness. This was when she needed her mother most but she knew that could never happen.

Abioye was out in the field when he heard someone call. 'Hi, neighbour!'

He looked up to see a man about his own age.

'Hi, how are you?

'Good, how are you getting on?'

'Just fine, really getting the hang of this farming.'

Abioye didn't want to reveal that he was the son of a king and would never have done such menial work at home.

The man walked over to him.

'Hi, I'm Bwana.'

'Hi, I'm Abioye.'

The two men shook hands.

It was sometime later that Bwana remarked, 'Congratulations, I see your missus is with child.'

'Yes, we are expecting soon.'

'Is everything all right?'

'Yes, I think so.'

'Look, there's a woman called Jahzara living not far from here who understands these things. Shall I get her to call?'

'Wait! Let me speak to Dalia first.'

That night, over supper of corn fritters and Sukuma wiki, he broached the subject.

'Darling, I was speaking to our neighbour about our new baby and he said that they had a woman called Jahzara who helped them when their child was born. She is knowledgeable about childbirth. She could come and help you with the delivery. Would you like that?'

'I had always hoped that my mother would be present at my first birth, but as she can't be…'

'I will ask her to call.'

A few days later there was a knock on the door.

'Come in.'

Standing at the door was a woman about the age of her mother.

'Dalia, I am Jahzara, may I come in?'

'Yes, please do, my husband told me you would be coming.'

'First of all, Dalia, may I congratulate you on your pregnancy. Is it your first?'

'Yes, I didn't have a show for many years after we were freed. I thought I would never have a baby, and then the miracle happened. I am so excited but saddened that my mother won't be here.'

'I understand. Did your husband explain to you what I do?'

'Yes, he said you assist at births.'

'Exactly, birth is a natural process. All of us have been born that way, so my job is to make sure that everything is going normally. I will call once a month to check on you and then nearer the time, come more frequently. I will be present at the birth but will simply watch provided everything is going well. You are a young woman and should not have any problems.'

'Thank you so much, Jahzara. You have made me feel so much better now that I know I won't be alone. Please come as often as you want. My door will always be open to you.'

The two hugged and Jahzara left

'How did it go?' said Abioye returning home later from a day on the farm.

'Fine, she is a lovely person, she reminded me of my mother.'

Chapter Thirty

Anika is Born

Abioye was on his way home and was near the house when he heard Dalia cry out. He rushed into the kitchen to find her holding her stomach.

'What is it, Dalia?'

'I think it's starting. I have just had a really strong contraction.'

'Shall I call Jahzara?'

'Oow! That was a painful one. No, let's wait a bit longer. I don't want to call her too soon.'

It was some hours later when Abioye was awakened by Dalia groaning.

'What is it dear?'

'I think you had better call Jahzara, the pains are coming more frequently.'

Getting dressed, Abioye rushed over to her house. The light was on in her kitchen. He looked through the window and saw that she was still up. He knocked. She saw him and beckoned him to enter.

'How is Dalia, is anything happening?' she asked, seeing his anxious look.

'I think you should come; the pains are becoming more frequent.'

A short while later, Jahzara knocked and came into the bedroom.

'Hello, Dalia, how's it going?'

'Hi Jahzara, thank you for coming so quickly, the pains are now coming every minute or so.'

'That's good, it won't be long now.'

Jahzara shouted, 'Abioye gets some hot water ready please, it won't be long.'

Having brought the water, Abioye waited outside, wanting to be by Dalia's side. Finally, he couldn't wait any longer,

He knocked on the door. 'May I come in? I want to be there,' he pleaded.

'Are you all right with that, Dalia?' asked Jahzara.

'Yes of course. Abioye, please come in, it's your baby also.'

One hour later, Abioye watched in amazement as their child emerged into the world. Immediately the silence of the night was pierced by a loud cry as their baby was born.

Jahzara handed him a pair of scissors.

'Abioye, would you please cut the umbilical cord?'

Their baby would be called Anika, meaning sweet-faced.

Chapter Thirty-one

Making Pottery

The arrival of Anika was a breath of fresh air to the family. And although Dalia was a natural mother, she missed her own mother. She imagined being home in Africa and seeing the joy on her mother's face at Anika's arrival. Abioye couldn't wait to get home to see her breastfeed their baby, marvelling at the strength of the little one's hold on life. Anika seemed to grow while he was watching her. In time he began to babysit while Dalia did her chores or visited friends.

Soon Dalia joined a group of other young mothers, meeting to share their experiences and to learn from each other. As the weeks passed, more and more mothers joined the group. They were homesick and needed something to remind them of their homeland.

It was Abioye who came up with the idea. They had just returned from sharing a meal with their friend Bwana and his wife Mariama. The spread was a traditional meal comprising Ugali and Sukuma wiki served from an earthenware pot. They were waiting to be served when Abioye noticed the earthenware pot.

'That's a fine-looking pot, Mariana, where did you get it from?' asked Abioye.

Bwana laughed. 'Tell them, Mariana.'

'I made it,' she said blushing.

'You made it? How?'

'It happened by chance. We had been out shopping in the market and I saw some pots on a stand. I remembered when I was a small child, I watched my grandmother make them. When I got home, I thought more about them and when Bwana came home, I asked him, 'Bwana, when you go to the farm tomorrow, will you have a look and see if there is any good clay? You often tell me that the soil is too heavy.' The following day he surprised me by bringing some home. It was ideal.

'You managed to make a pot?' Queried Dalia.

'Yes, eventually, but it took me a long time. You see, I couldn't remember the details but luckily there was a woman in the village who showed me. She was a potter and I sat with her, watching.'

'How did you manage it?'

'There are many ways, but she taught me how to make a coil pot. You can just take a lump of clay and shape it, scooping out the inside until you have a pot but it is very difficult to make it symmetrical. An easier way, and the method I used, was to make a coil pot.

'Coil pot? That suggests that you go round and round?'

'That's exactly what you do. You start by making a number of long thin rolls of clay. Next you make the base, a round flat disc. To make the sides you coil the rolls of clay around the edge of the base slowly building up the sides until the pot is tall enough. Then while the clay is still soft, you smooth out the rolls to leave flat inner and outer walls. Finally, you can decorate it while it is still soft and let it dry before firing.'

'I remember the decoration!' exclaimed Dalia. 'I saw the potters when I was growing up. I saw them taking strips of vegetation, winding them together and then using them to incise the surface of the pot leaving fine parallel lines.'

'Exactly.'

Some weeks later, Dalia plucked up courage to make her first coiled pot. She decorated it in the traditional West African style.

Epilogue

Two generations later, Anika's granddaughter Bikita would be born in Georgia, formerly a slave state of the United States. While playing in her garden, she would find a shard, a broken piece of pottery, half buried in the ground, the surface of which was incised with thin parallel lines.

References

Haour A., Manning K., Arazi N., Gosselain O., Gueye N S., Keita D., Livingstone Smith A., MacDonald K., Mayor A., McIntosh S., and Vernet R., 2010. **African Pottery Roulettes, Past and Present**, Oxbow Books, ISBN 978-1-84217-968-0